The New Adventures of Pippi Longstocking

The Storybook Based on the Movie

Based on a Screenplay Written by
KEN ANNAKIN

and Featuring the Characters Created by
ASTRID LINDGREN

VIKING KESTREL

VIKING KESTREL
Published by the Penguin Group
Viking Penguin Inc., 40 West 23rd Street, New York, New York
10010, U.S.A.
Penguin Books Ltd, 27 Wrights Lane, London W8 5TZ England
Penguin Books Australia Ltd, Ringwood, Victoria, Australia
Penguin Books Canada Ltd, 2801 John Street, Markham, Ontario,
Canada L3R 1B4
Penguin Books (N.Z.) Ltd, 182–190 Wairau Road, Auckland 10,
New Zealand
Penguin Books Ltd, Registered Offices: Harmondsworth, Middlesex, England

First published in 1988 by Viking Penguin Inc.
Published simultaneously in Canada

Copyright © Columbia Pictures Industries, Inc., 1988
All rights reserved
Photographs by Danny Feld
Library of Congress catalog card number: 88-50003
ISBN 0-670-82260-4

Printed in the United States of America by W. A. Krueger, Brookfield, Wisconsin

Set in Aster
1   2   3   4   5   92   91   90   89   88

Captain Efraim Longstocking

Tommy

Mr. and Mrs. Settigren

Annika

Alfonso

Pippi Longstocking

Mr. Blackhart

Miss Bannister

Rype and Rancid

The white sails of a high-masted schooner billowed against the sky, and the *Hoptoad* rose and fell on the swelling waves.

"Get those chests up here on the double," shouted Captain Efraim to the dozen sailors who were hurriedly loading the deck with large oak chests and bulging gunnysacks. His eleven-year-old daughter, Pippi Longstocking, stroked the back of a spotted white horse named Alfonso while she watched the commotion. Her hair was red as a carrot and was done up in braids that stuck straight out from her head. She had freckles all over her face, and her smile stretched from ear to ear.

That morning, Pippi was dressed like a pirate, with a black patch over one eye and a swashbuckling sword tied to her belt. Near where she was standing, one chest hit another and broke open, scattering jewelry and gold coins at Pippi's feet. She turned up her freckled nose and gave a ruby bracelet a disdainful kick.

"Papa, why do we want all this stuff?"

Pippi was not like most other little girls. She preferred her patched dress and long blue and orange stockings and oversized black shoes to jewels and finery.

"To keep you out of the stew pot,"

her father laughed. "Little-girl stew is a delicacy to the natives around here."

Even though Pippi Longstocking was one of the strongest girls in the world, she pretended to be scared and jumped into her father's arms.

"You'll protect me, right, Papa?" Pippi teased, playfully wrestling with him.

"Back to your lessons, daughter," he told her. "You should be learning your history and arithmetic with Fridolf."

But Pippi had scarcely begun her lesson when she heard her father shout, "Looks like a storm ahead!"

"Sorry, Fridolf, I can't study any more," Pippi said. "I've got to get up to the crow's nest."

She jumped on the horse's back and from there shinnied up the tall mast to the crow's nest almost at the top. Behind her came a small monkey dressed in blue pants, a bright red jacket trimmed with gold braid, and a little black hat.

"It's always good to have you around, Mr. Nilsson," Pippi said. Adjusting the sword on her belt, she stooped to pet the monkey. Then she took the spyglass and peered around her. Even as she watched, the weather on the horizon changed. A storm was brewing. Somewhere out in the ocean, a volcano erupted, causing huge swells and tidal waves. Suddenly, the ship began to heave from side to side in the gusts of wind, tossing everything helter-skelter. The sky turned black, lightning flashed, and torrents of rain began to fall.

"Papa, Papa, there's a big wave coming," Pippi shouted. "It's as big as the ship. It's coming straight at us!"

"Pippi, get down here, *now!*" Captain Efraim yelled back from the wheelhouse, where he was struggling to hold the wheel as it spun wildly about in his hands.

"I can't!" Pippi called back. "It's too close! Help me!"

"Lash yourself to the mast, girl. I'm coming up," her father called from below. The first mate took over the wheel.

The wind grew ferocious and the waves broke fiercely over the *Hoptoad*'s railing.

"I'm scared, Papa!"

"Hang on, for Pete's sake," her father shouted, pulling himself up the rope ladder. His voice cut through the scream of the wind. "And remember, if we get separated, swim toward Villa Villekulla. The Gulf Stream will take you there."

After a long while, the sea calmed and once again the sky turned blue. Pippi and Alfonso had managed to get aboard the raft with Mr. Nilsson. They were comfortably settled. Pippi had rigged a sail and Mr. Nilsson caught some fish.

Pippi offered Alfonso a fish but he shook his head disdainfully. Pippi stuffed it in her mouth and chewed it up, head and all. "When we get to Villa Villekulla, I promise I'll make pancakes with syrup three times a day," she said with a loud belch.

"You know, I wonder if I'll even recognize Villa Villekulla? It's been years since I've seen it—since Mama died."

Within moments, the crashing waves tore the sides from the schooner, and the sea's strong current dragged Captain Efraim in one direction and Pippi in another.

"Pippi, I'm drifting away," her father called hoarsely. "Remember, swim toward Villa Villekulla." And then he was gone.

Pippi struggled to keep her head above the swelling waves. Soon a raft floated by and Mr. Nilsson scurried aboard while Pippi grabbed onto Alfonso's tail and hoisted herself on his back. She clung to him for dear life.

Her heart ached a little as she remembered the time when her mother died and the Captain had whisked her off on the *Hoptoad* to sail the seven seas. They'd never returned. Pippi wiped her eyes with the back of her hand and drew herself up as tall as she could.

"We'll get to Villa Villekulla soon. I just know it. Pippi always comes out on top. And when Papa finds us, he'll say, 'Well done, guys.'"

It was a long day and a half before the raft finally washed up onto shore, and another half day until Pippi found Villa Villekulla.

The old house was right where it had always been, at the end of a road, and although it had taken Pippi a while to find it, she recognized it immediately. Since it had been neglected all those years, the garden was wildly overgrown with weeds and shrubs, and a massive gnarled oak tree had pushed its branches up and almost through the shingled roof. Behind the house was an old broken-down barn. Everything was in need of paint, including the picket fence which surrounded the entire property, with a padlocked gate in front. Pippi fell in love as soon as she laid eyes on Villa Ville-

kulla. There was lots to be done and Pippi loved a good project.

"Home at last!" she exclaimed as she lit the gas lamps in the old house.

While Pippi was lighting her lights, next door, in a neat and thoroughly modern house, Mr. and Mrs. Settigren had tucked in their children, Tommy and Annika, for the evening and gone out to dinner.

Tommy stared at the ceiling and sighed. "Mom says Villa Villekulla's more than a hundred years old. They can't just tear it down." He got out of bed, went to the window, and looked out across the lawn. "Annika, there's something strange going on over there tonight," he whispered. "There's all kinds of lights on."

"Who do you think is there?" Annika crept up next to him. "Maybe ghosts?" she said, shivering.

"Let's go see," Tommy whispered.

"No, not me!" Annika shook her head firmly.

Tommy grabbed a baseball bat from his shelf. "Don't be a sissy. I'll protect you."

They climbed the fence and tiptoed up the steps of Villa Villekulla's wood porch. The front door was ajar.

"See anything?" Annika asked, holding tight to Tommy's robe as he peeked through the crack.

"Shh," Tommy whispered. They tiptoed past the open door and climbed the first flight of stairs. "No, but you can't *see* ghosts."

"Then what are we looking for?" Annika asked.

Tommy didn't answer. He took her hand and they quietly tiptoed around the second floor, checking behind doors and furniture for anything suspicious. They had almost convinced themselves they'd imagined seeing lights when they pushed open a door at the end of the hall and a huge white *something* with black spots reared back and let out a loud whinny!

"A ghost!" Tommy shouted as they stumbled back down the stairs, only to land at the feet of another white ghost-like figure.

Luckily for Tommy and Annika, *this* ghost popped its head out of the huge white nightshirt and a freckled-faced, red-headed Pippi said, "Hi! Who are you?"

"You're not a ghost!" Annika announced, suddenly brave.

"Of course not. The ghosts live in the attic," Pippi replied.

"I know, we just saw one. He was big

16

and white and had four legs and was spotted all over," Tommy said as a shiver passed through him.

"That's Alfonso, my horse!" Pippi laughed.

"Horse? Well, what's a horse doing in an attic?" Annika asked.

"Beats me. I keep telling him not to go up there but he never listens." Pippi cupped her hands around her mouth and yelled up the stairs, "Alfonso! Get back on the porch where you belong."

Back came a complaining whinny.

"You see? He won't listen." Then Pippi extended her hand and helped both kids to their feet. "My name's Pippi. Pippi Longstocking."

Tommy and Annika introduced themselves and then Tommy asked, "What are you doing here?"

Pippi stood back on one of her long black shoes. She smiled her wide smile and her freckles seemed to glow in the dark. "It's *my* house, of course. I live here now," she said confidently. She turned away to light more of the gas lamps.

"Are you kidding?" Tommy asked, a

note of excitement in his voice. "You're going to stay here all by yourself?"

"Of course not. Alfonso and Mr. Nilsson live here too," Pippi said.

"Is Mr. Nilsson your father?" Annika asked. She didn't call *her* father "Mr. Settigren," even though that was his name.

Pippi laughed. "*This* is Mr. Nilsson," she said, introducing them to her monkey. "My father's a sea captain who was washed overboard in a storm."

"Did he drown?" Tommy asked.

"Of course not," Pippi said immediately. Then she turned away to hide her real concern and said, "He lives on an island and he's king of the cannibals."

"Cannibals? Real cannibals?" Annika asked.

Pippi nodded.

"There's no such thing as cannibals," Tommy blurted.

"How do you know?" Pippi cocked her head to the side and smiled a mischievous smile.

Tommy looked at Pippi closely for a moment and finally decided to believe her.

"And do they really eat people?" Annika asked, still not sure about Pippi's story.

Pippi gave them a spooky look and nodded. "Which reminds me, I'm starving! Are you guys hungry?"

"We're always hungry," Tommy answered.

"Who's for pancakes?" Pippi asked.

They followed Pippi into the huge kitchen and while she made them the best pancakes either of them had ever tasted, Pippi told them the story of how she came to be at Villa Villekulla without her mother or father.

"What is going on over there?" Mr. Settigren said as he pulled the car into their driveway. "Villa Villekulla's lit up like there's a party going on."

Mrs. Settigren ran into the house to

see if the children were asleep while Mr. Settigren hurried to Villa Villekulla. As he peered in the front window, he saw Annika and Tommy covered in pancake batter, prancing around the kitchen with a red-haired girl while all three stuffed food into their mouths.

"Tommy! Annika!" he shouted as he burst through the door, slipping and sliding across the floor straight into Alfonso.

He looked at the horse in horror. "What in blazes do you think you're doing?" Mr. Settigren sputtered at them. "What is all over the floor?"

Tommy and Annika couldn't say a word. They were too busy trying to gulp down their last mouthful.

"We're just having a midnight snack. Care to join us?" Pippi answered casually. She reached out her hand and helped him up.

"I've never seen such a mess. Tommy! Annika!" he shouted again. "Go home and get to bed at once!" And as Mr. Settigren pushed his children out the door, he turned and looked Pippi straight in the eye. "And as for you," he said sternly, "I don't know who you are or what you think you're doing in this house, but

I'll get to the bottom of this in the morning."

"Nice to have met you," Pippi called after them. Before she shut the door, she looked up in the sky. She could almost see her mother looking down through a peephole in the heavens. "Oh, Mama," she said with a deep sigh, "I already like it here so much. For the first time in a long time, I'm in a real home with a kitchen and my own bed. And I've made two new friends. We're having loads of fun together. But I do miss Papa. I hope he's safe. Please keep an eye on him, too."

Pippi closed her eyes to try and keep the tears from falling.

The next morning, Tommy and Annika could hardly wait for Mr. Settigren to go to work. The moment he left, they rushed back to Pippi's. Pippi had proclaimed it Scrubbing Day at Villa Villekulla and was bathing Alfonso. Soap and suds were flying everywhere. When she finished bathing Alfonso, Pippi dunked herself into the tub.

"Ah, nothing like a morning bath," she said.

"But you've got all your clothes on!" Annika cried in surprise.

"That's because it's laundry day, too," Pippi smiled. After a last dunk she stood up. "Of course there is such a thing as being *too* clean," she exclaimed as she

sprang out of the tub and did a somersault in the air, landing on her feet dripping wet and covered in suds.

"You'll catch your death of cold if you stand around like that," Annika said worriedly.

"Since when do people die from being wet?" Pippi looked confused. "But now that you mention it, I do remember one time at the North Pole. . . . I got so frozen after swimming with some seals and Eskimo kids, that I had to dry myself off like this . . ."

Then Pippi spun around like a top, so fast she was a blur to Tommy and An-

nika as they watched her spraying water and suds all over the kitchen. Finally she spun to a stop, bone dry. "See, that was easy. Now, how about a game?"

Since the place was already covered in soap and water, Pippi poured what was left in the tub onto the floor. Tommy and Annika roared with laughter. They hadn't had so much fun in ages.

"Rub-a-dub-dub, it's Scrubbing Day. My favorite day. Now that everything's soapy, we might as well scrub the floor, too." Pippi laughed. She strapped two scrub brushes to her feet and tossed two more to Annika and two to Tommy. Then

the three of them started to skate around the kitchen, singing gaily as they scrubbed everything in sight.

They were all having so much fun that they didn't even notice that Mrs. Settigren had come in until Annika skated straight into her arms.

"That's a fine method of cleaning. I must try it myself," Mrs. Settigren smiled.

Tommy introduced his mother to Pippi.

"Nice mom!" Pippi said as she held out her hand. "My mom is . . ."

But before she could explain, Mrs. Settigren hustled Tommy and Annika out the door. "Mustn't be late for the dentist," she called, waving a cheery good-bye.

Not long after Tommy and Annika had gone, a black limousine pulled up outside Villa Villekulla. Two slimy-looking fellows named Rype and Rancid helped a portly man, who was dressed all in black, out of the car. The man's name was Mr. Blackhart and he was a crafty land developer who wanted to buy Villa Villekulla and all the land it sat on. He was determined to have it, and if necessary he would go to any lengths to get the property.

"When I tear this old dump down there will be room for twenty units, and where the trees are, a pool!" he muttered to

his cohorts as he marched up the path to the house.

Mr. Blackhart was quite surprised and very angry when he saw a strange girl standing on the porch. He'd been assured the house was vacant.

"Good morning. Nice of you to call. I'm Pippilotta Delicatessa Windowshade Longstocking, daughter of Captain Efraim Longstocking—Pippi for short—at your service," Pippi said with a low bow. "What can I do for you? Selling vacuum cleaners? I'll take a dozen. Wrap them up."

"I'm not selling, I'm buying," Mr. Blackhart said, pushing past her through the front door. "And I want to buy this house."

"My house?" Pippi burst out laughing. "How can you buy a home? You can't wrap it, you can't carry it away, and you certainly can't fit it into your car. But since you probably don't make much money trying to buy houses other people live in, at least here's a little something for your trouble." Pippi reached into her pocket and pulled out one of her gold coins.

Mr. Blackhart looked closely at the coin. "Where'd you get this?" he asked, testing it between his teeth.

"I've got a whole mess of them under

the house. I just help myself whenever I need to."

Mr. Blackhart's eyes gleamed. "How did they get there?"

"Oh, that's a long story, but I can tell you this much: it's part of the treasure from King Solomon's mines." Pippi looked straight into Mr. Blackhart's eyes and smiled her mischievous smile. "I'm afraid you'll have to go now. It's wash day." And with that, Pippi picked up Mr. Blackhart like a wooden doll and carried him out of the house, down the steps, and placed him gently on the outside path.

"I'm sure you understand," she said sweetly. And before Pippi ran back in-side, she gave the amazed Mr. Blackhart a wide smile.

The next day, Pippi announced it was time to see the town. She got dressed up in a long yellow gown over her patched dress and a big floppy hat, and jumped on Alfonso's back. Tommy and Mr. Nilsson climbed onto a motorcycle and Annika, dressed all in rose, with a splendid boa around her neck, snuggled into the side car. They all sang as they sped along the highway to the center of town. There, they stopped in front of a tall building. A rather severe-looking woman was dragging a bunch of kids out of a bus and pushing them into a line.

"Get out of the bus, you little toads," the woman shrilled.

"Keep in line. No pushing," added a mean-looking girl, herding the children forward.

"That's no way to treat kids," Pippi said angrily.

"They're just orphans," Tommy replied, making a face. "Nobody wants them. Miss Bannister only brought them into town to have their hair cut and teeth pulled."

"All children should be wanted and loved," Pippi said sadly. "Especially if they have no mother or father. I know," she went on, brightening. "Let's go play with them!"

"We can't," whispered Annika, tugging at Pippi's sleeve. "Dad says we shouldn't even speak to them."

"That's ridiculous. They're just kids," Pippi said. She walked up to the crowd of children. "Who wants candy and ice cream?" she asked.

But before the children could reply, the head girl from the orphanage stepped in front of them.

"That's against the rules," she said coldly. "Who do you think you are, anyway?" She stared down at Pippi.

Pippi turned back to Tommy and Annika. She dipped into her bag and pulled out several gold coins. "Go buy ice cream and candy for all of them," she said. "We'll show them the time of their lives."

And with that, Pippi slipped off her long gown and started over to the toy shop. Five minutes later, she returned

carrying tin whistles, toy bugles, drums, and bells. Tommy and Annika were carrying two large boxes filled with ice cream and candies. Pippi blew on one of the bugles and shouted, "Come on, everybody, it's Pippi Longstocking Day." The orphans broke from their ranks and rushed over to the strange girl. Soon they were joined by all the other children in the area. Pippi, Tommy, and Annika began tossing ice cream and instruments to the outstretched hands, and the children screamed with delight. Soon a parade of children was underway, complete with marching band.

"Stop it! Stop it this instant," shrieked

Miss Bannister, attempting to drag two boys back into the barber shop. An ice cream cone went flying through the air and landed on her head. "Arrest someone. Arrest someone!" she screamed to a policeman standing nearby, as ice cream flew in all directions.

Above the ruckus in the street, in a second-floor law office, Mr. Settigren and Mr. Blackhart were calmly discussing the sale of Villa Villekulla.

"My wife says there's talk that Villa Villekulla used to be an old pirate hangout, but I've never heard anything about a treasure," Mr. Settigren said as he shuffled through a stack of papers.

"Well, there must be records—deeds or something. I want that place and I'm prepared to pay any legal costs involved to get it." The noise from the street below became so loud that Mr. Blackhart and Mr. Settigren dashed out of the office to see what was happening. Pippi, Tommy, and Annika saw the two of them coming toward them and took off running.

"Okay, Mr. Nilsson, time to do your stuff," Pippi called out.

The little monkey leapt on the motorcycle and pulled the gearshift as Pippi slammed on the kickstart. The machine growled to life as Annika and Tommy jumped on board. Pippi drove the motorcycle up a ramp beside a construction site. And they all sailed off into the air.

"Tommy! Annika!" Mr. Settigren called out, dodging the rain of ice cream cones.

"I know who's responsible for this," Miss Bannister said, shaking her fist.

"So do I!" replied Mr. Settigren angrily.

Mr. Blackhart staggered over. "You'll pay for this!" he hollered up at Pippi.

"Don't worry about them, Mr. Set-

tigren. When they're with me, they'll always come out on top!" Pippi called as they sailed over the crowd. Tommy and Annika waved to their father as the motorcycle dipped downwards and landed with a bump. The three children rode away singing. They were home safely by afternoon, just as Pippi had promised.

That evening before dinner, Mr. and Mrs. Settigren were discussing their unusual neighbor.

"Since Pippi arrived, I've never seen Tommy and Annika so happy," said Mrs. Settigren.

"And *I* never even see them anymore," Mr. Settigren sighed. "What happened to our peaceful little family?"

"You know, dear, Pippi told me she used to ride with her father on the Wall of Death in Bangkok . . ."

"And you believe that?" Mr. Settigren exclaimed. "Pippi's the biggest liar I've ever heard, and I'll tell you this, Miss Bannister is on the warpath. She'll get her way with Pippi yet."

Sure enough, the very next day, Miss Bannister arrived at Villa Villekulla.

With her hat planted firmly on her head and her purse slung over her shoulder, she marched toward the front stairs. Alfonso came out the front door just in time to greet her. Miss Bannister gave the horse a menacing look and cleared her throat.

"Whatever are you doing up there?" Miss Bannister asked in an unfriendly tone, glaring up at Pippi.

Pippi was on the roof peering through her spyglass.

"Looking for a storm," she answered pleasantly. "Why? Do you have some new game you'd like to play?" Pippi slid down the shingles.

"I'm afraid this will be no game," Miss Bannister replied.

Pippi rested her feet in the roof's gutters.

"I am a welfare worker for the county and I've found a place in the children's home for you," explained Miss Bannister.

"But I already have a place in a children's home," Pippi said, jumping down to the porch.

Miss Bannister looked confused.

"I'm a child and this is my home," Pippi said. "I'm already in a children's home, a very comfortable home, I might add. Thank you," she said politely.

"That's ridiculous," snorted Miss Bannister. "Children can't live alone. They have to go to school and learn reading, writing, and arithmetic."

"I can count enough to count my gold," Pippi smiled. "Our first mate taught me that while I was on board the *Hoptoad*. And as for the other stuff, I've gotten along just fine without it for eleven years. So, I'm afraid you'll have to get kids for your children's home someplace else."

Miss Bannister took a deep breath. "If you would kindly hold that beast, I would like to see what's going on inside."

"Well, all right, but not everything is in its usual place," warned Pippi. But Miss Bannister wasn't listening. Before Pippi could say another word, Miss Bannister had barged through the front door. Suddenly there was a terrible crashing sound.

"Somebody's always trying to steal my money," Pippi explained to poor Miss Bannister, who had run right into one of Pippi's burglar traps. She was lying across the stairs covered in flour.

Pippi walked over to her money chest and showed Miss Bannister her gold coins. "You see, if they get all my gold, then I might really have to go to that children's home with you."

Miss Bannister glared at Pippi. Pippi just smiled and handed her a bag of gold. "Say 'Thank you' to the townspeople for thinking of me, and please . . . buy the kids in the children's home some ice cream and marshmallows."

Miss Bannister tossed the bag of coins back to Pippi with a sneer, snatched her hat from Mr. Nilsson's head, and stormed outside and down the path.

Pippi hugged Mr. Nilsson and covered him with kisses. "I love you," she whispered, holding him close.

The next day, while Pippi, Tommy, and Annika picknicked in the huge tree next to Villa Villekulla, Mr. Blackhart and his men spied on them from across the road. Hitched to the back of their car was a horse trailer.

"Ah, there she is," Mr. Blackhart sneered. "Turning my property into a pigsty."

"It's not yours yet, boss," Rype said and grinned.

"No, but it will be soon." Mr. Blackhart grabbed Rype by the ear and led him back to Rancid. "Now, go do your stuff!" he ordered them.

Moments later, Rype and Rancid knocked on Pippi's door.

"Anyone home?" Rype called. "County Animal Control."

No one answered.

"Come to fix your livestock," Rancid called. Both the wormy fellows laughed. Then, looking around to make sure no one was watching, Rype and Rancid snuck into Pippi's house. One of them carried a rope and the other, a sack.

Pippi's money was lying all over the floor. When Rype and Rancid saw it, they gasped in delight. But as they reached down to touch the gold, a voice behind them warned, "Watch it! That's pirate gold. My Papa's king of the Kurrekurre Islands and put a curse on it. Anyone who touches the gold turns to dirt."

Rype and Rancid stared at Pippi in disbelief. Rancid pulled a piece of yellow paper out of his pocket. "We have orders to take your animals for shots," he whined.

"No one shoots my animals, or takes them anywhere!" replied Pippi.

"We're not going to shoot 'em, just give 'em jabs!"

"Not my animals," she exclaimed. She grabbed the two men by their collars, hauled them outside, and flung them into her bully tree. "You should be ashamed of yourselves for picking on a little girl," Pippi said.

As Rype and Rancid climbed down from the tree and tore down the path, Pippi called after them, "Sure you won't

stay for some chocolate creams and crumble?''

"You bungling idiots!'' yelled Mr. Blackhart. "All you had to do was *grab* that run-down horse and pesky monkey and she would have followed them to the ends of the earth. We would have had all the gold for ourselves!''

That night the Settigrens invited Pippi to stay for dinner.

"My papa and I've been shipwrecked so many times that there are only eight or nine islands in the world where we haven't been,'' Pippi said while she jug-

gled a few pieces of bread in front of her. Mr. Settigren eyed her, knitting his brows together.

"Weren't you scared?'' Annika asked.

"Well, there was that hurricane that made the peas fly out of the soup, and I did feel a bit queasy when the ship's cat came flying past me, stark naked. His fur landed on my fork.''

Mr. Settigren's eyes seemed to roll back in their sockets.

As Mrs. Settigren began to clear away the dinner plates, Pippi picked up the sugar bowl and sprinkled sugar all over the floor.

"Have you ever tried walking on sugar? It feels sensational between your toes,'' Pippi said, as she began to take her shoes off.

"Pippi! We don't do that kind of thing in this house,'' Mr. Settigren said. "Do I make myself perfectly clear?''

"Oh, sorry,'' Pippi quickly replied.

Then, trying to regain his composure, Mr. Settigren asked Pippi, "Tell me, what makes you think your father is still alive?''

"I know he is. You'll see. He always comes back.'' Pippi's voice trembled slightly. "He's got to.'' Just then, Mrs. Settigren brought in a spectacular dessert. Pippi made a quick dive and landed face-down in the yummy concoction.

"I can't see a thing,'' came Pippi's muffled voice. "Now we can play hide and seek.''

"That's enough,'' Mrs. Settigren said sharply, without her usual warm tone, and pulled Pippi into the kitchen. Her face looked angry as she cleaned the sticky mess from Pippi's face.

"If I promise to practice one half-hour a day, will you teach me all that table-manner stuff?" Pippi asked in a small pleading voice.

Mrs. Settigren smiled and her voice softened. "I will, if you tell me the *real* truth about where your mother is."

Without a pause, Pippi led Mrs. Settigren outside. "You see that cloud?" Pippi pointed up at the dark sky. "Well, there's a little hole in it right over my house and when I'm in trouble or need advice, I see her face. She always helps me, one way or another."

Mrs. Settigren put her arm around Pippi's shoulder. "I see," she whispered.

Pippi woke early the next morning and went to visit her new friend, Jake, and his wonderful flying machine, which he called an "autogiro." Pippi wanted to learn the secrets of flying and so she hid in the rear of the cockpit and watched closely as Jake switched on the ignition and swung the prop into action. The machine shuddered, sputtered, and then began shaking violently, causing poor Pippi to pop out of her hiding place.

"Get down! Down!" Jake called over the engine's roar. "They can take your head off!" He pointed to the propellers.

"Who cares? I ran into a headless pilot once . . . in Istanbul. He never knew which way was up!" Pippi said as she tried to steady herself.

Jake gently lifted Pippi out of the autogiro.

"I'm afraid you'll have to wait a few years to fly an autogiro. It's very dangerous."

But Pippi wasn't listening. Suddenly, she spread out her arms and went into a spin just like she'd done when she dried herself off on Scrubbing Day. Still spinning, she jumped a foot off the ground and actually stayed up for a full three seconds.

"That's it! That's the idea!" Jake's eyes widened in amazement.

"Is that all there is to it?" Pippi asked.

"Well, you'll need wings and a propeller but . . . yeah, you've got the idea."

Pippi's face was flushed with excitement and as she watched Jake take off in his autogiro, she yelled after him, "I bet I can do it, too!"

That night, while the rest of the world slept, Pippi went to work in the barn building her own version of Jake's autogiro.

The window next door slammed open.
"C'mon! Let's have some peace and quiet!" Mr. Settigren yelled.

Inside, Mrs. Settigren sat in bed, sadly listening to the little girl's industrious banging and hammering.

"Don't fuss. You're getting rid of her tomorrow, aren't you?" she snapped.

"You don't approve?" Mr. Settigren asked as he got back into bed.

"You know I don't. Not at all."

"A little girl can't live alone," Mr. Settigren said firmly and turned off the light.

Mr. Settigren did feel guilty the next morning when he handed Miss Bannister the document which would allow her to take Pippi to the children's home. Miss Bannister had gathered the police, the fire department, Mr. Blackhart and his cronies, and many of the townspeople to make sure Pippi was caught.

"Is all this necessary?" Mr. Settigren questioned. "I mean, she's only a child."

"A child! I've seen this child in action. Why, she's totally unpredictable," Miss Bannister shrilled. "No, we're all agreed. When Pippi's in the children's home, the town will breathe a sigh of relief."

Meanwhile, Pippi was accompanying

Tommy and Annika home from school. Once Pippi had tried to listen in on their lessons from outside the classroom window, but the teacher had shooed her away, saying that Pippi had to come inside if she wanted to go to school. Of course Pippi wouldn't do that! Suddenly, a school friend came running towards them. "They're coming for you! The police, the fire department, and Miss Bannister. Just about everyone in town is after you."

"I bet my father's in the crowd, too!" Annika said with disgust. The boy nodded. "Please come with us, Pippi," Annika pleaded. "We'll all run away!"

Pippi looked around as a police siren blared in the distance. The thought of adventure was exciting.

"How will we do it?" Tommy asked.

"I have the perfect solution," Pippi said with a grin. "Follow me."

By the time Miss Bannister and her brigade pulled up in front of Villa Villekulla, the barn doors were opening to reveal Pippi's newfangled giro contraption. While Pippi whirled with her arms outstretched, Tommy and Annika pedaled furiously in order to drive the makeshift propeller at the front of the flying machine.

"Up, up, up!" Pippi urged, as the thing rose from the ground, leaving Miss Bannister and the entire crowd staring in amazement.

Pippi and her friends flew for a while, finally landing in a lake surrounded by lush pine trees. They left the homemade giro floating near shore while they made camp under a tall pine. Pippi lit a fire

by rubbing two sticks together, as Annika and Tommy watched in awe.

"I'm too tired to hunt tonight," Pippi said as she tossed Tommy and Annika sandwiches from her knapsack.

"What would you have hunted, anyway?" Annika asked, smiling at Pippi's big talk.

"Oh, lions and tigers and . . ." Pippi paused, smiling mischievously. ". . . cannibals."

"Cannibals? Here?" Annika's voice shook.

Pippi nodded wisely, reached into her knapsack, and pulled out a long-handled pistol. "Just in case." She

winked as she disappeared into the tent. "Keep watch."

Annika moved closer to Tommy.

Hardly a moment passed before the brush near the tent moved. Annika and Tommy rushed in after Pippi.

"Pippi, there's something out there!"

"Probably a cannibal snooping . . ." Pippi laughed. "Looking through their cookbooks to learn how to make stew . . ."

Pippi stuck her head out of the tent. With a convincing "BANG! BANG!" Pippi imitated the sound of gunfire. "That should take care of them."

For the rest of the evening the three

but Pippi could find. They would leave in the morning.

When morning came, Tommy was the first one up and the first one to discover that their wonderful machine had sunk in the lake.

"How will we ever get back?" he asked worriedly. Annika began to cry.

"Who cares?" Pippi said. "I thought we were supposed to be running away." She grabbed hold of a rope-like vine, swung out into the water, and began to swim.

"Pippi, you've got all your clothes on!" Annika admonished, sniffing back the tears.

"I know. It's more fun this way."

Tommy and Annika laughed, shed their clothes, and jumped into the cold clear water.

"It's freezing," shrieked Annika as Tommy and Pippi merrily splashed her.

"I'm a sea monster," bellowed Pippi as she dove underwater and pulled on their toes. They were too busy swimming and splashing to notice a cow back on shore that was calmly eating all their clothes.

"Next time, be like me and swim with your clothes on," Pippi advised, while helping her friends concoct clothing out of blankets and bits of cloth from Pippi's knapsack. Soon they were able to move onward, singing cheerily as they followed a winding river. Suddenly they came upon an old beer truck that had tipped over, strewing barrels everywhere.

friends entertained each other by telling how life would be when they all became pirates together. The full moon shone down on them as they talked of freedom and adventure. The same moon shone down on a group discussing plans of a different sort.

After Miss Bannister and her search party had spent a fruitless day hunting for the runaway children, Mr. Settigren had enlisted the aid of Jake, the flying inventor. Jake agreed to take Mr. Settigren in his autogiro to places no one

"We're saved," Pippi exclaimed, rolling an empty barrel to the river's edge. Before you could say "Pippi Longstocking," the three of them were drifting downstream, each in a floating barrel.

"This is as safe as taking a Sunday stroll," Pippi bragged. "I knew a guy once who went over Niagara Falls in a barrel. He said it was fantastic."

Bobbing along with the current, they gaily resumed their singing. Gradually their speed began to increase and the barrels started to rock and spin through the water as if they were on a roller coaster.

"What'll we do?" cried Annika, clutching the sides of the barrel.

Just at that moment, from over a ridge of trees came the whir of Jake's autogiro. As the machine leveled off over the river, Jake and Mr. Settigren could see that only a short distance ahead of where the barrels floated, the river narrowed and crashed over a great roaring waterfall.

The speed of the barrels accelerated even more. Pippi's exuberance vanished. Her freckles appeared to darken as her face turned white with fear.

"Grab hold of my barrel, Tommy,"

she commanded as she grasped Anni-ka's barrel firmly with both hands.

"Don't worry. We'll come riding out on top like we always do," called Pippi, smiling bravely.

The autogiro followed above and Mr. Settigren lowered a rope ladder. Pippi gripped the rung tightly, hooked Annika under her free arm, and told Tommy to climb onto her shoulders. Hanging suspended above the falls, they watched with horror as the three barrels were sucked over the edge and smashed onto the jagged rocks below.

The shaken and bedraggled children

arrived home to find Miss Bannister and her cohorts waiting to take Pippi off to the children's home.

"Wouldn't you like some gold coins instead?" suggested Pippi, without her usual gusto.

"Pippi, dear, you can't go on like this," said Miss Bannister in a patronizing tone.

"Can I ride in the fire engine?" asked Pippi, attempting to stifle a yawn.

"Yes, yes," replied Miss Bannister. "Anything. Now come." She firmly guided Pippi towards the children's home van.

"Well, okay," Pippi sighed in a sleepy

little-girl voice. "Maybe just till Christmas." And she crawled into the van and fell asleep.

The weeks dragged by as a miserable Pippi attempted to adjust to life in the children's home. She hated the uniform they made her wear. She hated not being able to wear her tight braids. She couldn't make any sense out of her teacher or her classroom.

"Pippilotta—if that's really your ridiculous name—please tell me, how much is twelve plus fifteen?"

"If you don't know something as simple as that, you shouldn't be teaching," Pippi answered.

The other children in the classroom gasped.

"I won't stand for rudeness in this class." The teacher jumped to her feet.

"Then please sit down," Pippi answered simply.

Miss Messerschmidt whacked Pippi's fingers with a ruler and made her sit in a corner the rest of the day.

Nighttime in the dormitory was even worse. When Pippi tried to tell stories about her travels to faraway places like Australia, the children laughed at her.

"You're nothing but a big liar. Our teacher even says so," the head girl taunted her.

Pippi couldn't understand what made the kids stay in a place like the children's home. None of them ever seemed happy.

"Well, they give us food and shelter," a little girl said. "And sometimes, if we do what we're told, they're nice to us."

Pippi just shook her head sadly. She didn't understand.

One day, when Pippi was alone in the dormitory, she was staring out the window and caught sight of the familiar hole in the sky.

"I hope you're not busy up there, Mama, playing that harp and all . . . but you know what your Pippilotta has been going through. Why do they ask so many questions when they already know the answers? I'm so confused. If only Papa were here." Pippi paused for a moment and waited for an answer.

"What? I didn't quite hear that, Mama."

She listened again.

"What? Send Papa a message? But how?"

Again, Pippi listened.

"In a bottle!" Pippi brightened. "Okay, Mama. Thanks. I'll give it a shot," she smiled. "You can go back to playing your harp now."

Pippi knew what she had to do. That night, she braided her hair. Then she tore off the regulation nightgown that covered her colorful patched dress. Finally, she grabbed her old oversized shoes and slipped out of the dormitory.

Once she was on the landing, Pippi wondered which was the safest escape route. Downstairs she could see the housekeeper and the janitor, playing cards. Down the hall she could see the iron gate that barred the front door. Above her, in the attic, she noticed a flickering light.

Although she knew it was risky, Pippi chose to climb the dark and creaking stairs to the attic. Dust and cobwebs lay thick around her. When she arrived at the top of the stairs, she cautiously pushed open the attic door. Something flapped past her head and a rat scurried across the floor. As Pippi's eyes adjusted, she saw a room filled with broken beds and piles of rubbish. As she made her way slowly toward the open window, a shadow rose behind her. Just as Pippi reached the window, somebody pounced on her, placing a hand over her mouth.

"Shh! What are you doing here?" a man's voice whispered.

Pippi struggled to turn around. Even in the dim light she could tell he had a beard and long greasy hair. He smelled terrible and his face was filthy. He had bundles of cans slung over his shoulders.

"What are *you* doing here?" Pippi asked defiantly. "You're definitely not a ghost."

"I climbed up," the man said.

"A ladder?" Pippi asked, peering out the window.

"No, I came up the wall."

Pippi laughed. "You tell bigger whoppers than I do. Only flies walk up walls."

"And spiders and lizards and me!"

"Prove it," demanded Pippi.

The man smiled and opened one of the tins slung over his shoulder. "I'm Greg of Gregory's Gripping Glue," he explained while he spread the sole of his shoe with glue. "This is very special glue I invented. It grips when you want it to and lets go when you no longer need it to stick." Then the man carried his shoes over to the wall and planted them about three feet up.

"Come." He beckoned to Pippi and carefully lifted her into the shoes. "Now just walk up the wall."

"I can't," Pippi protested.

"Of course you can. You can do almost anything if you believe you can."

Pippi smiled. "That's what I used to think."

"Then think it again," answered the glue man.

Pippi slowly lifted one foot and then the other, moving slowly up the wall.

"Look, I can do it," she shouted, walking upside-down across the ceiling. "Thump, thump, thump."

Hearing the noise, the janitor came up to the landing below. With a burning cigarette hanging from his mouth, he looked around suspiciously. "The rats around here sure get bigger all the time," he said, tossing the cigarette on the floor and stomping back downstairs.

"I've got to go now," Pippi said. "Can I use this glue?" she asked, already smearing it on the bottoms of her shoes.

"Sure. But if you want, I'll take you down with me in the morning," the glue man offered with a yawn.

"That'll be too late," Pippi answered. In her stocking feet she clambered over the junk pile and found an old wine bottle with a cork.

"Can you write?" she asked, holding out a pencil and paper she'd tucked into her pocket.

The glue man nodded.

"I can't," Pippi said. "But I need a very important note written. Will you write it for me?"

"With pleasure," the glue man said, taking the pencil and paper. He wrote as she dictated.

"PIPPILOTTA IN JAM POT. COME QUICK TO VILLA VILLEKULLA."

"Thank you," murmured Pippi as she fingered the precious note. She gently folded the paper into the bottle and sealed it with the cork.

"Good-bye," Pippi called, climbing out the window, carrying the bottle and wearing the sticky-bottomed shoes. She hesitated for a moment when she saw how far she was from the ground.

"Keep believing, Pippi," the glue man called softly from above. "Keep believing."

Cautiously Pippi made her descent. When she was a few feet from the ground, she untied her shoes and somersaulted, landing upright in her stocking feet. She waved to the glue man and then skipped away, singing all the way to the beach.

At the beach, she found the tallest

sand dune and stood looking out over the water. Pippi kissed the bottle for good luck and flung it into the sea.

"Find it soon, Papa," Pippi whispered. As she slowly turned from the beach she saw with horror that the sky was red with flames.

"The children's home," Pippi exclaimed, rushing back to the big old house she had just escaped from.

By the time Pippi got back to the home, the townsfolk had all gathered to watch the firemen fight the fire. The janitor had already pulled one group of children out. Tommy and Annika and Mr. Nilsson had arrived and they were looking everywhere for Pippi.

The crowd grew larger.

"How many more inside?" one of the firemen hollered.

"There's another two . . . and that Longstocking girl," Miss Bannister added.

No sooner had Miss Bannister said Pippi's name than she appeared.

"Pippi, how did you get out?"

"My mother lent me her wings and I flew down," Pippi laughed. Mr. Nilsson hopped onto her shoulder, chattering a mile a minute he was so glad to see her.

"Can't you ever stop making up stories? Even at a time like this?" Miss Bannister snapped.

Suddenly, the glue man appeared at the top window with the two children who hadn't made it out with the rest. Four firemen ran over with a net and pulled it taut.

"Jump!" yelled the crowd.

But the two terrified children only cried and clung to the glue man. Desperate, the glue man began to spread glue on the bottoms of their shoes and tried to convince them to walk down the wall. The children only shook their heads and covered their eyes. Attempting to teach them how the glue worked, the glue man lost his balance and plummeted down, landing safely in the net.

"Jump!" repeated the crowd. But the two children just stood at the window and cried louder.

Pippi thought quickly. She grabbed a rope from the fire truck and climbed halfway up a nearby telegraph pole with Mr. Nilsson on one shoulder and the rope coiled over the other.

She fastened one end of the rope to

the top of the pole and the other to Mr. Nilsson. Then she threw Mr. Nilsson toward the window.

Mr. Nilsson landed safely on the sill. He wrapped the other end of the rope around a pillar until it was tight. Pippi braced herself and yelled, "Don't worry, kids, just pretend we're playing circus." Like an expert tightrope walker, Pippi made her way carefully across the twenty-foot gap between the pole and the window. The two kids stared at her in amazement when she jumped onto the windowsill.

Quickly, Pippi put the girl under one arm and the boy under the other and started back across the rope. Twice she had to take a backward step for balance but finally made it across. As she reached the pole, Pippi said, "Now for the second part of the game. It's called 'Down the slippery pole.' All the firemen play it."

Zoom went the children down the pole as the crowd cheered.

"Mr. Nilsson, come out!" Pippi called from her roost on the pole. "I don't want roast monkey for supper."

The timbers began to crack, and a beam fell as the flames licked closer to the window. Then a furry hand appeared on the sill and up popped Mr. Nilsson's head.

"Mr. Nilsson, come here at once," Pippi called again.

But the little monkey was frozen with fear and could only shake and moan.

Without a moment's hesitation, Pippi raced across the rope. Mr. Nilsson's tiny outstretched arms grabbed her and hugged her close.

"It's okay," she soothed, noticing the rope beginning to burn. "Just hang on." With that, the rope snapped and Pippi grabbed the end, swinging them both right into the middle of the net.

The crowd cheered, "Give her a medal!"

And Pippi cheered too. "Three cheers for Pippi of the South Seas and for Mr. Nilsson, the bravest monkey in the whole darn world!"

"Pippi, I'm so proud of you," Mr. Settigren said as he rushed toward her.

"I think I've misjudged you," Miss Bannister said, almost shyly. "What can I do to make it up?"

"Just let me go back to Villa Villekulla. Mr. Nilsson and Alfonso really miss my pancakes. They want me home."

Pippi was granted her wish and they spent the next weeks making themselves comfortable at Villa Villekulla once again. Christmas Eve found Pippi balancing on top of a chair putting the finishing touches on a rather straggly Christmas tree. Mr. Nilsson and Alfonso watched approvingly. In the distance they could hear muffled laughter and cheers from the Settigrens' party next door. Pippi came down from her perch and leaned her face against the cold windowpane.

"Merry Christmas, Tommy and Annika," she said sadly, trying not to feel left out. "And you, Pippi, Merry Christ-

mas. And you, Papa," she added. "I hope you're happy and eating lots of lovely cakes and things on your South Seas Island. I love you."

A look of doubt crossed her face as she peered up at the sky.

"You sure he's not up there with you, Mama? You know, I mean, you would tell me, wouldn't you?" Pippi sighed. "I miss you both, terribly."

Pippi turned to Alfonso and Mr. Nilsson. "I guess Christmas is family time. We're lucky to have each other, guys." The animals nuzzled close to her as Pippi wiped the tears from her eyes.

Suddenly, from outside, Pippi heard singing. When she rushed out on the porch, she saw lanterns and lots of people coming toward Villa Villekulla. Mr. and Mrs. Settigren were leading their whole party across the lawn. Tommy and Annika skipped on ahead. When they all halted, Miss Bannister stepped out in front.

"Happy Christmas, Pippi dear. We all want you to know we love you and are thinking of you."

"It's small now, but it will grow," said the head girl from the children's home as she handed Pippi a large cardboard carton.

When Pippi opened the carton, a small brown and white puppy licked her face. It had a big red bow around its neck.

For once Pippi didn't know what to say. She cuddled the dog while everyone cried, "We love you, Pippi. Please stay in our town forever!"

Mr. Settigren grinned as he stepped

forward and presented Pippi with an ancient scroll, bound with a ribbon.

"What is it?" Pippi asked, untying the ribbon.

"It's the deed to your house," Mr. Settigren announced proudly. "I had to go back a long way, but I checked the records and Villa Villekulla is truly yours. People like Mr. Blackhart can't bother you anymore."

"Hip hip hooray!" cheered the crowd. Pippi smiled from ear to ear, her freckles glowing.

Christmas morning, Tommy and Annika came over to open packages with Pippi. As they were crumpling the last piece of paper, they heard singing outside.

"We live on the seas, no apologies . . ."

It was Captain Efraim Longstocking, and under his arm he carried an enormous duffle bag.

"Oh, Papa, you've come back!" Pippi cried, jumping into his arms.

"Would I ever let you spend Christmas without me?"

"I knew you hadn't drowned," Pippi grinned, giving him a big hug.

"Me? Drowned? I could no more drown than a camel thread a needle." He roared with laughter. "First they wanted to eat me, but when I tore down a palm tree with my bare hands they changed their minds and made me king. From then on I ruled in the mornings and built a new *Hoptoad* in the after-

noons. I was already on my way to find you when I fished out that bottle."

"Are you really a *cannibal* king?" Tommy asked.

Captain Efraim nodded. "But there's no danger anymore—I converted the natives. Now they are vegetarians."

"You don't look like a king," Annika said.

"I have my robes in my bag," Captain Efraim told them.

"Put them on, please, Papa," Pippi pleaded.

Behind the stair railing, the children hid their eyes while Captain Efraim slipped into his costume. They opened their eyes in astonishment to see him standing fully clothed in his long robes, holding a spear in one hand.

He boomed out, *"Ussamjussar mussoz filibissor!"*

"What does that mean?" Annika asked in awe.

"It means *'Tremble, my enemies!'* When I sailed away, the island folk fell on their knees chanting *'Usamajura jussomkara,'* which means *'Bring her back soon or we'll have your guts for garters!'* " Pippi's father laughed.

"Bring who back soon?" Pippi asked.

"Who do you think?" Captain Efraim teased. "They only let me leave when I said I'd bring back a princess named *Pippilotta!"*

Pippi took a flying leap and landed once again in her father's arms. "Me? A princess? You really *are* the best papa in the whole world. I'm going to be a princess of the Kurrekurre Islands!"

Tommy and Annika tried to hold back their tears as they watched Pippi's excited reunion with her father.

The whole town joined them to see Pippi off. As the *Hoptoad* readied itself to sail, the crowd on the dock waved sadly.

"At least she'll be looked after by her father," Mr. Settigren said, taking out a handkerchief. "We often forgot that

Pippi is just a little girl and helpless, really."

"Helpless? Pippi?" Miss Bannister and Mrs. Settigren said together.

As Pippi peered at the group through her father's spyglass, she saw Tommy and Annika. Both of them looked sad. Annika was crying.

Slowly, Pippi turned to her father and said, "You know, Papa, I forgot to say good-bye to a lot of nice people."

"Well, girl, open up your lungs and shout," Captain Efraim said.

Pippi shook her head. "You know, I want to be with you more than just about anything in the world," she said slowly. "And I'd really like to be a princess. But I can't bear to see people crying, especially because they'll miss me."

Captain Efraim put his arms around Pippi, and for a moment his eyes looked sad.

"I want to try a few new things here, Papa. Maybe even school," Pippi said softly.

Captain Efraim smiled. "As always, you're right, Pippilotta. I'll miss you lots, but in my heart I know it's best for a child to live an orderly life."

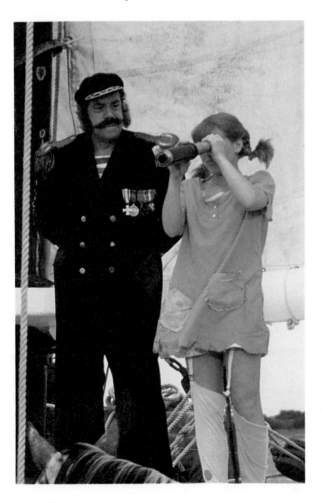

"Especially if that child can order it for herself!" Pippi laughed.

And with that, Pippi waved to the crew, picked Alfonso up, and tossed him back into the sea. Then with a flying leap, she landed firmly on Alfonso's back with Mr. Nilsson resting comfortably on her shoulder.

"I'll come back and visit," called Captain Efraim, waving to his daughter. "Just go on being yourself, Pippilotta!"

"I will. You can rely on that," Pippi called back. "Never fear, Pippi will always come out on top!"